· THE ·
MASTER
VIOLINMAKER

Paul Fleisher

Photographs by
David Saunders

HOUGHTON MIFFLIN COMPANY · BOSTON · 1993

Thanks to James R. Allen, Elisabeth Anderson,
Lanny and Barbara Anderson, Kellie Bethke,
Jacklyn Boney, Nicole Kelleher, and Charnette McGill
for their help in the completion of this book.

Printed in the United States of America

WOZ   10   9   8   7   6   5   4   3   2   1

Library of Congress Cataloging-in-Publication Data

Fleisher, Paul.
    The master violinmaker / Paul Fleisher ; photographs by David Saunders.
        p.   cm.
    Summary: Photographs and text document the creation of a violin
by master violinmaker John Larrimore.
    ISBN 0-395-65365-7
    1. Violin—Construction—Juvenile literature.   2. Larrimore, John—
Juvenile literature.   [1. Violin—Construction.   2. Larrimore,
John.]   I. Saunders, David, 1952-   ill. II. Title.
ML802.F56   1993   92-28050
787.2′1923—dc20   CIP
                    MN AC

For Debra   — P. F.

John Larrimore makes violins, violas, and cellos. For six years he worked as an apprentice to a master violinmaker. Many years earlier, his teacher had learned violinmaking as an apprentice, too. In this way violinmakers have passed on their knowledge for hundreds of years.

By the time Larrimore finished his studies, his teacher had already retired. When Larrimore finished his apprenticeship, his teacher gave him all his old violinmaking tools. It was a very special gift. Some of the tools are more than one hundred years old!

Now Larrimore has his own little shop, on a shady side street in Richmond, Virginia. He's an expert violinmaker himself—a master of his craft.

The best violins are made by hand, not by machine. It will take Larrimore hundreds of hours to make a single instrument. He starts by choosing just the right pieces of wood.

The back, ribs, and neck of a violin are made of maple. Maple is hard and strong.

The top of the instrument is made of spruce. Spruce wood is strong, but softer than maple.

The pieces of wood that a fiddlemaker uses can't have any knots. The grain—growth lines that run through the wood—must be straight and even. Otherwise the violin would crack or bend out of shape.

Larrimore is very choosy about the wood for his instruments. He only uses wood that grows in New England. The cool climate of Vermont and New Hampshire causes trees to grow slowly. This makes the wood strong.

As wood ages, the water in it dries and the wood shrinks and hardens. Wood for a violin must be completely dry. Otherwise, the violin will warp. Larrimore uses wood that has dried for at least twenty years.

A violinmaker judges the age of a board by its color. As wood ages, it gets darker. A board that will make a good fiddle isn't always pretty. The board might look rough and stained. Larrimore has one special piece of maple, given to him by his teacher, that is chocolate brown. It's about 125 years old!

Once Larrimore finds a piece of wood that he thinks will make a good fiddle, he gives it one more test. He holds the board between his thumb and finger. Then he taps it and listens. The best pieces of wood ring like a bell when he taps them. When Larrimore hears that clear, pure sound, he knows he's found a good piece of wood for an instrument.

Larrimore starts with the back of the violin. With a pattern called a template, he traces the shape of half the violin on the maple board.

Then he flips the template over and draws the other half. This ensures that one side of the violin is exactly the same shape as the other.

With a thin-bladed coping saw, he carefully cuts the outline of the violin from the wood.

The board starts out about four centimeters thick. Larrimore shaves wood away with cutting tools called planes. The planes peel the wood away in thin, curling strips.

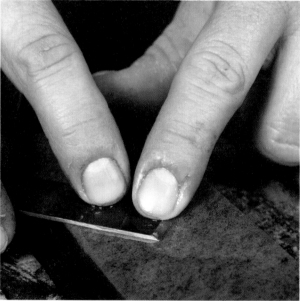

The planes must be kept very sharp. After every fifteen or twenty strokes, he stops to sharpen the blade on an oilstone.

After every few cuts, he checks his work. Is the shape right? Is the wood thin enough? Larrimore measures the wood's thickness with calipers. He checks the curve of the wood with arching templates.

Shaping the back of the violin takes about twenty hours of work.

He keeps cutting away wood until the back of the violin is curved and very thin. In most places it's no thicker than a nickel.

But the hard old maple is strong. The curved shape makes it even stronger, just as the arch in a bridge helps support the roadway above it.

To make the top of the fiddle, Larrimore splits a wedge-shaped piece of spruce in half.

He glues the two halves together, back to back.

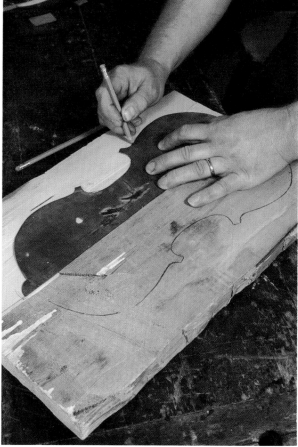

With the template he draws the shape of the violin again. The glued line goes right down the center of the instrument.

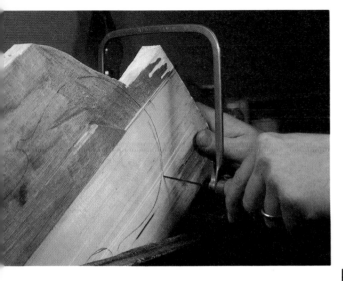

He cuts out the top of the violin with the coping saw.

Then he uses planes to shave away the wood, little by little. Every few minutes he stops to sharpen the plane. After about twenty more hours of work, the arched top of the violin is just the right thickness.

To finish shaping the top and back of the fiddle, Larrimore trims the last slivers of wood away with tiny razor-sharp thumb planes.

Then he smooths the surface of the wood with sharp pieces of broken glass.

He cuts graceful, curving f-holes into the top of the violin. A violin is just a wooden box with strings. When a musician bows the strings, the air inside the box vibrates with sound. The f-holes allow the sound to come out.

The size and shape of the f-holes are very important. If they are too big, the violin will be loud but harsh-sounding. If they are too small, its sound will be too soft.

Now it's time to make the ribs, or sides, of the violin. With a band saw Larrimore cuts long, thin strips of maple. Each piece is about three centimeters high and only three millimeters thick.

Then he planes the maple strips until they are only about one millimeter thick!

He shapes the maple strips around a hot bending iron. Heat allows the wood to bend without cracking. Larrimore bends the ribs to fit the shape of a wooden mold.

He glues the ribs to small spruce corner posts and clamps them into place. As the wood cools, it hardens in the outline of the mold.

He uses a special glue made from the hide and hooves of horses. Violinmakers have used hide glue for hundreds of years. It holds wood together without soaking into it. That keeps the glue from spoiling the sound of the instrument. Hide glue also lets a violinmaker take a fiddle apart to be repaired.

Larrimore glues the back of the violin to the ribs. When the glue dries, he removes the mold.

Larrimore carves a long strip of spruce to fit against the inside curve of the top. This is the bass bar. It strengthens the left side of the fiddle and gives it a deeper, richer sound.

Then he glues the bass bar into place.

He glues the top of the fiddle to the ribs.

The neck of the violin is also made of maple. Larrimore cuts out the rough form with a saw.

Then he shapes the neck with carving tools and planes.

He carves the scroll at the end of the fiddle's neck. Each violinmaker puts some special touches into the design of his scrolls, to make them just a little bit different from anyone else's.

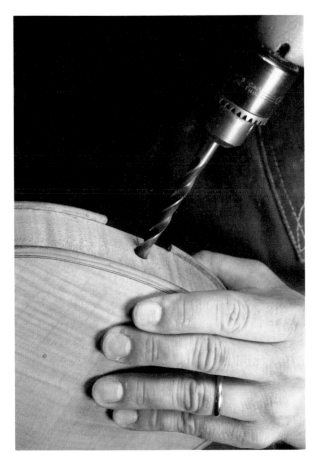

Larrimore cuts a small notch in the end of the violin and glues the saddle into place. The saddle is made of hard ebony wood. It will support the tailpiece when the violin is finished. He also drills a small hole in the end of the violin. Later, that's where he'll install the end button. The tailpiece will be attached to the end button with a stiff plastic loop.

Varnish protects wood from moisture and also makes it look beautiful. After the violin is glued together, Larrimore covers the wood with about thirty-five thin layers of varnish. He spreads each coat of varnish on with a small, stiff brush.

After each coat, he hangs the violin up to dry for a
whole day.

Larrimore makes the thick, stretchy varnish himself. It's made from linseed oil, turpentine, plant gums, and pigments. The ingredients are "cooked" together at a low heat for several days before the varnish is ready to use. The varnish must be just right. If the varnish is too stiff or thick, the violin won't vibrate properly. Its sound would be ruined.

Just varnishing a violin takes more than a month.

After each coat dries, he rubs the violin with a rough cloth to remove extra varnish. The cloth is manmade sharkskin. In earlier times, violin-makers used real sharkskin to smooth the finish.

Larrimore finishes the instrument with two or three coats of clear varnish. He polishes the last coats with oil and fine powdered stone, called pumice.

There's no varnish on the neck. That would make the violinists' hands stick, so they couldn't play as fast. Natural oils from the musicians' hands protect the wood of the neck. That's why the neck of a violin is a lighter color than the rest of the instrument.

A violinmaker doesn't work on just one instrument at a time. While he's waiting for the violin to dry, Larrimore fixes instruments that people have brought to his shop, or he works on other fiddles that he's building.

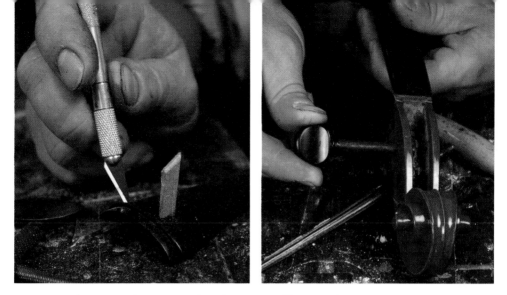

A violin needs several other small wooden parts. The
tuning pegs, fingerboard, end button, nut, and tailpiece are
made of ebony, a very hard, black wood. Ebony grows in
tropical rainforests. Larrimore makes these parts from pre-cut
pieces called "blanks." He carefully shapes each blank to fit
his instrument exactly and puts each small piece into place.

Although the bridge of a violin is very small, it's also very important. It doesn't just hold up the strings; it also carries their sound to the rest of the instrument. Larrimore carves the bridge from a small piece of very hard maple.

Although he knows how, Larrimore doesn't usually make the bows for his fiddles. There are other people who specialize in the craft of bowmaking. Larrimore relies on them to make the bows for his instruments.

Larrimore carves another small piece of spruce to fit inside the fiddle, between the top and the back. This is the sound post. It carries sound from the top of the instrument to the back, so the whole instrument will vibrate. It also strengthens the right side of the instrument.

Larrimore puts it into place through the f-hole with a special curved tool. He uses a tiny light and mirror to look inside the violin to check his work.

At last, he can string the violin. The top string is made of steel. The others are nylon wrapped with aluminum or silver. He listens to the fiddle and makes small adjustments to make it sound even better. He moves the sound post and bridge to just the right spots. He might even have to take the fiddle apart and shave off a little more wood here or there.

Finally, the violin is ready for his customer. It sings with a strong, sweet voice. The wood seems to glow with its own inner light. If it is well cared for, people will enjoy listening to its beautiful sound for hundreds of years to come.

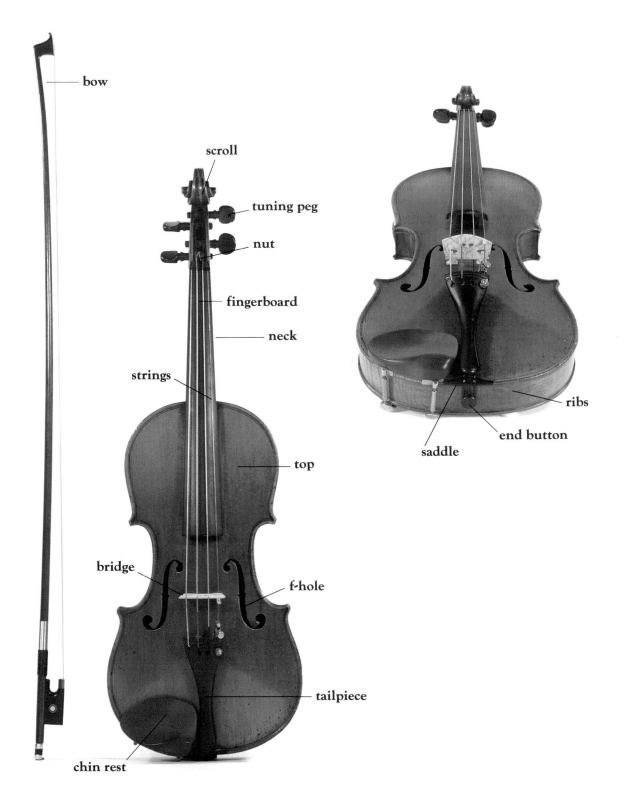

bow

scroll

tuning peg

nut

fingerboard

neck

strings

top

bridge

f-hole

tailpiece

chin rest

ribs

end button

saddle